Dear Parent:
Your child's love of reading starts here!

Every child learns to read in a different way and at his or her own speed. Some go back and forth between reading levels and read favorite books again and again. Others read through each level in order. You can help your young reader improve and become more confident by encouraging his or her own interests and abilities. From books your child reads with you to the first books he or she reads alone, there are I Can Read Books for every stage of reading:

SHARED READING
Basic language, word repetition, and whimsical illustrations, ideal for sharing with your emergent reader

BEGINNING READING
Short sentences, familiar words, and simple concepts for children eager to read on their own

READING WITH HELP
Engaging stories, longer sentences, and language play for developing readers

READING ALONE
Complex plots, challenging vocabulary, and high-interest topics for the independent reader

ADVANCED READING
Short paragraphs, chapters, and exciting themes for the perfect bridge to chapter books

I Can Read Books have introduced children to the joy of reading since 1957. Featuring award-winning authors and illustrators and a fabulous cast of beloved characters, I Can Read Books set the standard for beginning readers.

A lifetime of discovery begins with the magical words "I Can Read!"

Visit www.icanread.com for information
on enriching your child's reading experience.

For Ernie, who
sometimes lets
me write.
—C.B.

To Blake, the
greatest of great
nephews!
—Uncle Troy

Clarence was just a muddy pickup.

One day, there was a big storm.

Lightning zapped the car wash.

Now Clarence has a secret.

Water turns him into Mighty Truck!

I Can Read Book® is a trademark of HarperCollins Publishers.

Library of Congress Control Number: 2017954074
ISBN 978-0-06-234470-0 (trade bdg.) — ISBN 978-0-06-234469-4 (pbk.)

18 19 20 21 22 SCP 10 9 8 7 6 5 4 3 2 1   ❖   First Edition

MIGHTY TRUCK

THE TRAFFIC TIE-UP

BY *CHRIS BARTON*   ILLUSTRATED BY *TROY CUMMINGS*

HARPER
An Imprint of HarperCollinsPublishers

Stella was Axleburg's news chopper.

It was her job to fly way up high.

From there, she told what she saw.

"YAY, MIGHTY TRUCK!" yelled Stella.
"HE SAVED THE LOAD OF PAINT!
THE AXLEBURG ART SHOW CAN
GO ON!"

In the sky, Stella had to be loud.

It was the only way to be heard.

She did not need to be loud inside.

But she was used to being loud.

"THAT BOOK IS GREAT!" Stella yelled.

"PLEASE PASS THE POPCORN!"

"I HOPE I DIDN'T WAKE YOU!"

7

Clarence could not stand it.

He had a strong opinion.

He could not keep it to himself.

"You are too loud," Clarence said.

"Try using your inside voice."

"MY WHAT?" shouted Stella.

"I DON'T THINK I KNOW HOW!"

"I'll show you," Clarence said.

Clarence's best friend was Bruno.

Bruno was making art for the show.

Clarence took Stella to see him.

Bruno was busy drawing.

Clarence spoke in a whisper.

"How's it going?" Clarence asked.

"Pretty well," Bruno said softly.

Surf wagon Mr. Dent loved art, too.

Clarence and Stella visited him.

Mr. Dent was painting.

Clarence kept his voice to a hush.

"It's looking nice," Clarence said.

"Thanks," Mr. Dent said quietly.

His cat let out a low purr.

Outside, Stella thanked Clarence.

"Now I understand," Stella said.

"I'll start using my inside voice."

14

"You can do it," Clarence said.

The next day, traffic was awful.

Why hadn't Stella told anyone?

But she had.

They just couldn't hear her.

16

"There's been a crash," said Stella.

"It will take awhile to clean up."

Stella was using her inside voice.

But she was using it outside.

"I'm late!" said one artist.

He was trying to go to the art show.

"Me, too," said another.

"We're *all* late," said a third.

They wished Mighty Truck could help.

Clarence did, too.

But he could not see how.

"See!" Clarence said.

"That's it, everyone!

Let's all clean our windshields.

Maybe we will *see* a way out."

Window cleaners squirted.

Wipers splashed the stuff all over.

It got all over Clarence.

He got totally wet.

Clarence became Mighty Truck.

"All right!" said Mighty Truck.

"Let's go!

Stella's too quiet!

And traffic's too slow!"

Mighty Truck borrowed a balloon.

He tied his radio to the string.

The cord stretched.

And stretched . . . and stretched.

It finally reached the chopper.

Mighty Truck turned up the volume.

"Stella!" Mighty Truck said.

"Inside voice, please," said Stella.

"We're outside!" said Mighty Truck.

"And we can't hear you!"

"Is it OK to be loud?" she asked.

"Clarence said I shouldn't be."

"Please be loud!" said Mighty Truck.

"I'll talk to Clarence in private."

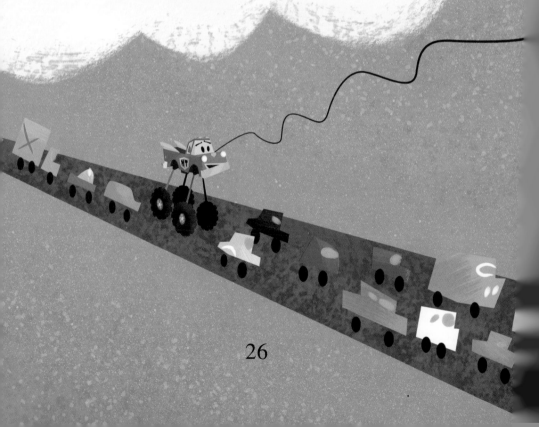

Mighty Truck gave Stella his radio.

It gave her extra volume.

"TRAFFIC IS TIED UP!" Stella said.

"BUT WE'RE WORKING IT OUT!"

Stella did her job at full blast.

She was loud and clear.

The art show could start on time.

And Axleburg went back to normal.

Only two things were different.

One was Mighty Truck.

He got a new radio.

The other was Clarence.

He still had opinions.

There were still things he disliked.

But he learned that saying so

didn't always help.

Clarence's friends showed him their art.

"What do you think?" they asked.

He did not like it at all.

But he chose his words carefully.

Even when it was *mighty* hard.